YOU'RE THE MAIN CHARACTER. YOU MAKE THE CHOICES.
CAN YOU SURVIVE?

P9-DJL-163

Howard Pyle's
MERRY ADVENTURES
of
ROBIN HOOD

adapted by
Brandon Terrell

Minneapolis, Minnesota

Dedication

To my sweet Stella.

Edited by Ryan Jacobson
Cover art by David Hemenway
Cover logos by Shane Nitzsche

10 9 8 7 6 5 4 3 2 1

Library of Congress Control Number: 2012949757

ISBN: 978-0-9821187-3-3

Dear Reader,

What's better than reading a good book? Reading one where you make the choices! This isn't just any Choose Your Path adventure, though. It's a retelling about one of my favorite childhood heroes: Robin Hood.

As a boy, I had a bed with two drawers beneath the mattress. This raised the bed higher and also created the ideal secret spot to read. I would shimmy under the bed with a book, a pillow, and a light, and I'd read for hours. One of the stories I read in my "secret fort" was *The Merry Adventures of Robin Hood* by Howard Pyle.

The tales were filled with familiar names: Little John, Friar Tuck, and the evil Sheriff of Nottingham. Howard Pyle created a wonderful story for readers, one full of adventure. I've taken great care to stay true to his original storytelling. However, please consider this a shortened introduction to the world of Robin Hood.

When you feel ready, I encourage you to search out the work of Howard Pyle and read the original story of the famed Sherwood Forest outlaw. Until then, I hope you enjoy my interpretation of the character. Huzzah!

—Brandon Terrell

How to Use This Book

As you read *Howard Pyle's Merry Adventures of Robin Hood*, you will sometimes be asked to jump to a distant page. Please follow these instructions. Sometimes you will be asked to choose between two or more options. Decide which you feel is best, and go to the corresponding page. (But be careful; some options will lead to disaster.) Finally, if a page offers no instructions or choices, just turn to the next page.

Enjoy the story, and good luck!

Table of Contents

Prologue:
The 3:45 Train

You hurry down the subway stairwell. You need to catch the 3:45 train back to your neighborhood.

"Excuse me. Can you spare a dollar?" It's a man's voice, and it sounds cracked and defeated. It drifts up from the bottom of the stairwell.

As you reach the entrance of the subway platform, you see the man. He is leaning against a nearby wall. His clothes are tattered and dirty. Beside him, a white, plastic grocery bag bulges with his belongings. An old mug sits almost empty, just a few coins and a crumpled dollar in it.

You make eye contact with the man. His eyes are sad.

"Can you spare a buck?" he asks you.

Frightened, you shake your head and speed away. Your hand reaches into your jeans pocket to the money there. Of course, you have cash. You just sold your used comic books, so you can buy a new skateboard. But you don't want the stranger to know this.

You use your subway pass to get onto the platform, and then you find an open bench to wait upon. You spy a digital clock on the wall. It's 3:37 p.m.

You try to forget about the man, but it's hard not to glance over your shoulder at him. The third time you turn around, he sees you looking. He lifts one dirty hand in a wave.

You do not return the gesture.

"Excuse me, is this spot taken?" A woman points to the bench beside you. She is older, with graying hair and a large handbag,

You shake your head, and she sits, digging in her bag for something. She removes a few items: a book, lip balm, and her keys. She places the book beside you on the bench. It's an old hardcover. The title, printed in gold letters, reads *The Merry Adventures of Robin Hood* by Howard Pyle.

The chimes of an arriving train fill the platform. It's not your train yet, but the woman beside you stands and joins a small crowd near the platform edge.

Go to the next page.

You notice the faint sounds of cheering crowds, of clanging metal, and of music—is that a harp? It's all coming from somewhere nearby. Glancing down, you see that the woman has forgotten her book. Those sounds seem to be coming from between its pages!

Puzzled, you lean down. You prod the book with one finger. Curiosity fills you. What will happen if you pick up the book—if you crack open the cover? Nothing? Something thrilling? Or perhaps something dangerous and sinister?

The woman's subway train clatters into the station, drowning out all other sounds. Soon, the book's owner will be gone. Will you open the book? Or should you find its owner? What will you choose to do?

To open the book, go to page 41.

To return it to its owner, go to page 66.

These guards have trained with the best swordsmen in England. To flee from them could be the last thing you do in life. Instead, you drop your axe and raise your hands above your head.

One of the riders dismounts and wraps thick rope around your wrists. His knots are tight. Then he climbs aboard his horse and ties the other end of rope to his saddle. He turns back in the direction of the Great North Road, and he leads you away.

As you stumble along, the forester rides to your right. He says, "Did you think your actions would have no consequence? The reward for poachers is far greater than twenty marks." He laughs and gallops ahead.

Soon, the sun disappears beneath the horizon. The guard with the torch says, "Riding this late wasn't our plan. It took longer than expected to find the poacher."

"We must make camp," says the second guard, "or risk our horses getting hurt on a fallen log or in a hole." And so they stop to discuss their options.

A twig snaps in the nearby woods, and you are immediately alert. You scan the shadows, yet you see no movement.

Suddenly, your group is swarmed by men moving in the darkness. The lead guard drops his torch in surprise. One of the silent attackers smothers the flame. Swords are drawn, and the guards swipe blindly.

A stranger appears beside you. You see a glint of metal in the moonlight as he uses a dagger to slice the rope from your hands. "Come," he whispers. "Follow me."

You shed the rest of your rope and follow him into the dark woods. The going is slow. At times, you must strain to see him ahead. But at last, you reach an outcropping of rocks, and he stops.

"We'll wait here," he says.

You feel confused and scared. Who is this man? One of the outlaws rumored to roam Sherwood Forest? They are nothing but a myth. Aren't they?

Others soon join you. In all, twenty men meet at the outcropping.

The man who rescued you asks, "What of the guards?"

A thin man responds. "We sent the cowards on their way. They're likely a mile north by now."

Another man lights a torch, and you get your first good look at the group. They are clad in green. Some carry bows and have quivers full of arrows at their backs. Others carry swords or daggers. Two men hold the dead deer between them. Despite their weapons, you are no longer frightened. If they meant you harm, you'd be dead by now.

"Who are you?" you ask.

The men chuckle.

The stranger who cut you free proclaims, "We're the outlaws of Sherwood, known as the Merry Men." He offers a hand. "I'm Will Stutely."

"The Merry Men? You're real?"

Will claps you on the shoulder. "Indeed we are."

You shake his hand. "Robin. Formerly of Locksley."

"You're a fine shot, Robin. I saw your contest with the foresters this morning. Later, when one of our men saw two guards riding with a forester, we followed."

"Why did you save me?"

"You don't deserve to die for your actions. Now, come with us."

Will leads the way. It's clear that he knows Sherwood well, even in the black of night. The others follow in a line, as you move through the depths of the forest.

Eventually you hear voices, laughter, and the soft sounds of a harp.

Will stops. "There it is," he says.

At the bottom of a hill, in a hidden forest clearing, a small band of men and women are gathered around a fire. The men who saved you join them, accepting hugs and handshakes.

"Who are they?" you ask.

"Others like you," Will answers. "Outlaws and runaways. Some were caught shooting deer to feed their families. Others were servants who escaped from cruel masters." He looks at you and smiles widely. "Welcome to the Merry Men of Sherwood Forest, Robin Hood!"

Go to page 59.

You turn to the forester. Masking your voice, you reply, "I have just one prize in mind this day, and it's a golden arrow."

The forester laughs. "Well, then I hope you fair well, stranger." With this, he returns to the striped tent.

The bugle sounds again, and it's time for the second round. Each man fires two arrows. The crowd watches without a sound.

When your turn arrives, you see the tall stranger watching you from just inside the tent. You decide it's best not to draw attention to your skills. You aim your shot near the target—but not at its center.

When your arrow strikes, it lands beside the finest shot of Gill of the Red Cap. You have done just enough to remain in the contest. Your second arrow mirrors the first, landing so close to the other that a cheer arises from the crowd. Many toss their caps into the air for joy over such marvelous shooting.

Now three men are left: you, Gill of the Red Cap, and an archer named Adam O'Dell. The crowd offers shouts of praise for both of your competitors. Very few call out for Jack of Teviotdale.

Adam O'Dell is first. His hands shake as he fits an arrow into the string and releases his final shot. It strikes the target near the outer edge, far from the center. Groans erupt from the crowd.

Gill of the Red Cap is calm as he draws an arrow, fits it to the string, and fires. It strikes the target just a hair from the center.

"Gilbert! Gilbert!" chants the crowd.

"Now that's a good shot!" cries the Sheriff from his perch. "I believe the prize is yours and rightly won!"

Gill removes his cap and bows before the Sheriff.

It will take all of your skill to best the archer. As you step forward, the crowd laughs at you. To them, the shooting match is over. Some are already gathering their belongings and beginning to leave.

You spy Marian, still watching, and you take a deep breath. Drawing the bow, you string an arrow and pull it back. As you release the arrow, the bow gives forth a deep musical twang.

The arrow arcs beautifully across the range. It drives into the target at the spot that marks the very center. The shot is so true that it cuts a feather from Gill's arrow.

No one speaks a word. Instead, each man, woman, and child stares at you in amazement.

Into this silence, the announcer's voice booms, "The winner!" He blasts three times upon his bugle.

The crowd bursts into cheers. Above it all, you hear the roaring voice of Little John. Gill of the Red Cap throws his bow and arrows in anger.

The announcer leads you across the range to the Sheriff, who stands and approaches you. Spectators crowd around to see the man who shot so well.

"Here, good fellow," the Sheriff says in a pinched voice. He holds one palm upward, and Sir Guy of Gisbourne hands him the golden arrow. "Your prize so rightly won. What is your name, archer?"

You consider drawing back your hood. It would be a joy to see the look on the Sheriff's face as he learns his enemy has won his contest. But to do so would place your life in danger. Instead, you respond, "Men call me Jack of Teviotdale."

"Then, in the name of King Henry," the Sheriff says, "I proclaim Jack of Teviotdale to be the fairest archer my eyes have seen. If you will join me, we shall feast together. And I shall try to convince you to join my army. What do you say?"

You can hardly believe what you're hearing. The Sheriff has not only asked you to dine with him, but he has also asked you to become a member of the King's Guard in Nottingham. You want nothing more than to take your winnings and return to Sherwood Forest. But saying no to the Sheriff could be a big mistake. Should you accept the Sheriff's offer or decline it? What will you choose to do?

To accept the Sheriff's offer, go to page 93.

To turn down the Sheriff, go to page 84.

Your hasty decisions have often landed you in trouble, but you feel sure that today is not one of those times. Your mind is set.

"I'll attend the shooting match in disguise," you tell the others. "I'll shoot for the golden arrow. If I win it, we'll share its wealth with the poor and needy."

"Hurray!" shouts the band.

"Some of you will disguise yourselves as friars, some as peasants. All will carry a good bow or sword, in case the need should arise. Will you follow me?"

The Merry Men shout in support. And so you gather your bow and arrows. You put on a tattered robe with a large hood. On your left eye, you place a leather patch. The disguise is so good that even Little John needs a moment to recognize you.

The rest of the Merry Men hide their identities as well, and you set off along the Great North Road.

It is nearly noon when you reach Nottingham. The town is a fair sight to see. A row of benches stretches along the meadow beneath the town wall. Across from the benches, a railing has been placed to mark the boundary for peasants to stand. Between the benches and the railing, a shooting range stands fifty paces wide. At one end is the target; at the other, a tent of striped canvas. Near the target, a raised seat is decorated with ribbons and flowers. This spot is reserved for the Sheriff of Nottingham.

The benches have already begun to fill with noblemen, knights, and squires. Many of the poorer folks sit upon the green grass near the railing. It is time for your companions to go their separate ways.

You gaze across the range while your Merry Men take their places in the crowd. Little John stands in his friar robes. David of Doncaster, a slim man with a scar on his cheek, leans against a rail. His bow is hidden beneath loose beggar's clothes. Yet it is the young woman beside him who makes your heart nearly stop.

"Maid Marian," you whisper.

The beautiful maiden stands in the grass, among the poor folk. She wrings her hands with worry. What is she doing here? Perhaps she heard of the Sheriff's plot to capture you and is here to warn you. Perhaps she holds some important piece of information about the day's event. Or maybe she is bait, part of the Sheriff's plan to find you.

You wish to go to Marian, to let her know that you're here and to learn what she might know. But is it too risky? What will you choose to do?

To speak with Marian, go to page 28.

To ignore Marian, go to page 74.

The path to the west offers more shelter, and it places greater distance between you and the foresters. But there is something wrong about the stone trail. Something dangerous. You'll take your chances going north.

You remove your quiver and its arrows from your back. Without your bow, the arrows are of no use. As you hold the arrows, you think of the shooting match in Nottingham and of the sweet Maid Marian. You will probably never see her again.

You cast the half-empty quiver in the direction of the western trail. Then, on legs that burn and ache, you begin to climb the path back into the forest. The footing is treacherous, and the going is slow.

You hear voices to the east and the snap of a branch. "Here! I've found the boy!"

You search the trees uphill until you discover the source of the voice. One of the men—a thin fellow—is pointing at you. He grips a sword in his other hand.

Quickly, you rush along the path, hoping that his companions are far behind him. A fallen tree blocks the trail ahead. It's too high to jump over, yet not nearly high enough to crawl beneath.

When you reach it, you leap into the air. Your stomach strikes hard against its jagged bark. As you try to scurry over the log, an arrow strikes, just missing your leg. A second whistles over your head.

You fall back onto the path with a thud. The air is forced from your lungs. For a moment, you can barely breathe. The men are almost upon you. You have no choice but to hide. You might be able to slide below the downed tree.

From behind, a dirty hand snakes out and clamps over your mouth. You try to scream and struggle. It's no use. Your captor is quite strong.

"Hush," he hisses into your ear.

You twist in his arms until you feel the blade of a dagger pressed against your throat.

"Stop squirming," the man whispers. "I'm trying to save your life."

You've heard stories of outlaws hiding in the depths of Sherwood Forest. The stories say that they steal back what the Sheriff and his men have taken. Their legend gives hope to the poor. Is this man one of them? If so, is he risking his life to save you, or is he about to rob you?

He pulls you along the trail, toward your enemies. Then he turns and drags you toward the rocky hillside.

No, not just a hill. You notice the entrance to a cave. It's anyone's guess what fate might await you inside. Should you trust this man and go into the cave? Or should you break free? What will you choose to do?

To enter the cave, go to page 56.

To escape from your captor, go to page 83.

You cannot speak with the forester. It's too risky. So you remain with your back to him.

"You, boy," he says. "Why won't you answer me?" He puts his hand on your shoulder and roughly turns you. Before you can stop him, he pulls off your hood, revealing your face.

The forester's eyes widen. He grabs the leather eye patch and snaps it from your face. "The child outlaw from Sherwood!" he exclaims. Then he seizes your cloak and yanks you forward.

"Sheriff!" he shouts.

The Sheriff stands as the forester wrestles you onto the range. "What is this?" asks the Sheriff.

"I found an outlaw among the archers."

The Sheriff stomps over and grabs your chin to study your face. "It's you," he snarls, "Robin Hood!" Then a smile crosses his face. "Ladies and gentlemen!" he cries. "I have before me the famed outlaw, Robin Hood!"

The crowd gasps as the Sheriff picks up a nearby club. He draws back his weapon and swings. It connects solidly behind your right ear. Pain erupts in your head, washing over you. And then the world goes black.

You wake to see the cold, stone walls and metal bars of a prison cell. You shake your head to clear it. Your tongue feels like sandpaper against your lips.

A small window in your cell offers just a sliver of light. It shines weakly against your face. The walls of the cell suddenly feel like a coffin. It's hard to breathe.

You fall onto the floor, your back resting against the metal bars. This is how your life will end. Sitting here. In the dark. Alone.

Go to page 67.

You quickly remove the horn from your belt. You move it to your lips, but the towering stranger swats it out of your hand. He draws back his weapon and swings. It connects solidly behind your right ear.

Pain erupts in your head, washing over you. And then the world goes black.

Go to the next page.

You wake to see the cold, stone walls and metal bars of a prison cell. You shake your head to clear it. Your tongue feels like sandpaper against your lips.

A man lurks in the shadows of the hall outside. You strain to see him better, and he steps into the nearby light from a window. It's the Sheriff of Nottingham.

A black cloak is pulled tightly across his armored chest. Dark hair curls about his face. His gray eyes stare at you. "The famed Robin Hood," he says. "You chose a strange place to slumber. Three of my guards happened upon you." He laughs cruelly. "Now, you are mine forever! Enjoy your stay, Robin Hood." With that, the Sheriff turns and stalks away.

The small window in your cell offers just a sliver of light. It shines weakly against your face. The walls of the cell suddenly feel like a coffin. It's hard to breathe.

You fall onto the floor, your back resting against the metal bars. This is how your life will end. Sitting here. In the dark. Alone.

Go to page 67.

You've been away from your love for too long. You would give anything to let her know you're safe. So you hurry across the range.

"Maid Marian of Locksley," you say.

When she sees you in your disguise, she does not immediately recognize you. But then her eyes light up. She steps through the crowd.

Bugles sound across the range. You glance back and see archers exiting the tent. The Sheriff rides across the range on a white stallion.

Suddenly, a guard is at your side. "You there, archer," he commands. "Get along with the others." The guard grasps you tightly by the collar and pulls you away.

Marian cries out, "Robin!"

Your heart plummets inside you. Has Marian just given you away?

The guard turns you around. He inspects you closely, then tears the eye patch away with a snap. "Guardsmen! To me!" he barks, snatching the bow from your hands.

Quickly, you rush to the wooden rail, leap over it, and fall hard upon the ground. The wind rushes from your lungs, leaving you dazed.

You are met by a guard like no other. He wears a horse's hide from neck to boots. His face is hidden by a terrible mask. The sword in his hands is the largest you've ever seen.

He steps to you and swings his sword. You narrowly dodge it. He spins and strikes again. But this time, it connects with your stomach.

You struggle to breathe. There is Marian, sobbing. There is Little John, rushing to your aid too late. There is the Sheriff, laughing at you. And there is the mighty swing of the guard's sword. And then there is nothing.

Go to page 67.

The western path provides more shelter than the one winding north. Fearful of an arrow striking you in the back, you choose the safety of the boulders.

The gap in the rock wall is narrow, so you remove your quiver and its arrows from your back. Without your bow, the arrows are useless anyway. But as you hold the arrows, you think of the shooting match in Nottingham. You remember the sweet Maid Marian, whom you will probably never see again. You toss the quiver toward the northern path. It lands on the hard-packed earth and tumbles, end over end. Its contents scatter.

On legs that ache, you move along the rocky trail. You go as quickly as you can, but you twist through passages so tight that you must hold your breath to fit. You're relieved when the path widens and you see the end of the rocks. But there's one problem: The path ends in a twenty-foot drop to the river below.

Voices echo from the main path. The foresters have found your quiver. Hopefully, they'll think you went north, but you cannot be sure.

The boulders to your right look like they can be climbed. If you can make it across and reach the trees on the other side, you'll lose the men for sure. Taking a deep breath, you swing your left leg onto the cliff wall and find a rock to step on. Your fingers dig into a small crack, and you pull yourself onto the cliff. Slowly, you slide along the cliff wall. The river rolls and roars below.

The stone beneath your right foot gives out. Your left foot slips, and your hands scramble to find something—anything—to grasp. For the briefest of moments you hang by one hand. The strain on your fingertips is too much, and you are forced to let go.

You crash into the cold river. It tears the breath from your lungs, and you are instantly numb. All sense of direction is lost. The current whips you around and pushes you against your will. Your head dashes upon a large rock.

The world begins to fade away, and you realize with dread that the river will be your final resting place.

Go to page 67.

You turn to face the foresters. Without thinking, you slide the bow down your arm and into your waiting hand. Fear and rage swim through you as you string an arrow. You aim for the trunk of an oak tree behind the large forester—just to scare him. Yet as you release the arrow, the bearded man lumbers forward, directly into the arrow's path.

Your shot strikes him just below the left shoulder. He cries out as blood begins to stain his clothes. The man falls forward, face-first onto the ground.

"What have I done?" you mutter.

There is no time to consider this. You must escape. Before the others realize what has happened, you crash through the trees, into the depths of Sherwood Forest.

"Get the boy!" shouts the tall man.

Your heart is sick, and you are afraid. Adrenaline pushes you. You rush onward, as low-hanging branches tear at your face and arms.

Behind you, the men pursue. Arrows slice through the forest, lodging into nearby trees. You arrive at a small path and turn sharply onto it. The move is so sudden that you drop your bow to keep from falling down.

You run for nearly a mile into the wilderness. The foresters stay on your tail, but they fall farther behind. You slow your pace, moving carefully and quietly.

Ahead, you notice the sounds of water crashing against rock. Moments later, you reach the edge of a cliff. You look down and see a flowing stream twenty feet below. You could jump. But without knowing the depth of the water, it's too dangerous.

Since you can no longer continue forward, you must make a decision. You can go north, where the path winds upward, back into the forest. This route will bring you closer to the men who pursue you. Or you can go west, where the path cuts through rocky terrain, along the cliff's edge. There, the risk of falling is great. What will you choose to do?

To move north, go to page 21.

To move west, go to page 30.

The risk is too great, even for you. You watch as the large man is led to the Great North Road. Moments after the guards pass the tavern, two more riders appear at the edge of town. You walk back into the tavern, relieved that you didn't make a horrible mistake.

Yet you cannot get the image of the captive out of your head. You do not know the man, but you believe that he would be a great ally. You only wish your Merry Men were here with you. If so, you could have made a different choice.

Pushing back your plate, you exit the tavern and rush into the woods. You stomp through the glades and along a narrow pathway.

As luck would have it, you come upon a team of Merry Men, led by Will Stutely. You smile widely and say, "I'm glad to see you. Five of the Sheriff's men ride along the North Road. They have a prisoner, a man who would make a fine Merry Man!"

Will nods. "Then let's go and get him."

You and the Merry Men hurry through the forest until the sun is nearly setting. When you reach the North Road, you hope that you've arrived ahead of the guards.

You wait an hour, until the sound of hooves drifts across the wind. Five guards approach. The large stranger staggers along behind them, his head bent to the ground.

As they climb the stony road, you step out from your place in the undergrowth and block the path. "Release your captive," you say.

The guards look to one another. Then they burst into laughter that echoes through the woods. "And why should we do this?" the first guard asks.

You smile. "Because you're surrounded by twenty men with arrows pointed at you."

At once, the Merry Men release a flurry of arrows. None are meant to strike, but they do their job: scaring the Sheriff's men. The riders quickly release the prisoner. Then they turn and gallop away.

You watch them go, and when all is safe, you untie the large man.

He looks at you with surprise. "You? You're the one from the bridge!"

"I am," you respond. "My name is Robin Hood of the Merry Men."

"Robin Hood?" he gasps. "You're full of surprises."

He looks at the many gathered men. "The outlaws who steal riches from the wealthy to help the poor?"

You clap him on the shoulder. "How would you care to join our ranks, good sir?"

The stranger laughs. "After what you've done for me, I would join you gladly."

"Then we've gained a good man today. What name do you go by?"

"I'm John Little."

Will, who enjoys a good laugh, speaks up. "Oh yes, little you are indeed."

Go to the next page.

And so, with John Little at your side, you plunge into the forest, retracing your steps until you reach camp. There, great fires are built, and a feast is held.

At one point during the meal, Will stands behind the enormous John Little and proclaims, "It is now time to welcome our new man!"

The gathered men and women chant, "Aye! Aye!"

Will Stutely raises his glass over his head and pours its contents over John's head. "From now on, you shall be known as Little John!"

The outlaws cheer and holler. At first, you believe John to be angry. But then he tilts back his head and laughs loud enough to scare away the birds in the branches above.

3

The Shooting Match

Little John proves to be a valuable member of the Merry Men. He soon becomes your best friend. He trains others with a staff and leads hunting parties on a regular basis. They often return with their kill slung over his broad shoulders.

Your bad dreams continue to wake you early, and this summer day is no exception. You decide to test your bow by traveling into the woods alone. There is a small brook near the southwest edge of Sherwood, where herds of deer are known to stop and drink.

A crash sounds in the forest nearby. You spy a young man—a child younger than you—dashing toward camp. He's out of breath when he reaches you.

"What is it?" you ask.

The boy swallows a lungful of air. "Along the Great North Road. Men on horseback. Archers."

"There are many archers in England," you answer.

"They spoke of a contest. A grand shooting match in Nottingham. The winning prize is a golden arrow."

Little John lumbers over. "What's the commotion?"

"The Sheriff is hosting a shooting match," you say.

Little John shakes his head. "This shooting match is a trap. The Sheriff wishes to lead you there."

"Then he shall not see me," you say with a smile. "Wake the others, John."

The outlaws are roused from their sleep and are soon gathered together.

You step atop a large boulder and speak to them. "Merry Men, the Sheriff of Nottingham has proclaimed a shooting match. The prize is a bright golden arrow. It is a prize we would gladly have."

Despite your excitement to be in the contest, you know it's a risky idea. Perhaps there's a safer way to bring the golden arrow back to Sherwood. After all, you could always sneak in and steal the arrow.

All eyes are upon you. You must decide your course of action. Will you go there to win? It is possible to do so in disguise. Or would it be better to steal the arrow with your Merry Men? What will you choose to do?

To attend the shooting match, go to page 18.

To steal the arrow, go to page 46.

Whatever adventure the book presents—and however dangerous it may be—the opportunity is too great to pass up. You snatch the book off the bench. It is heavier than you expect, and you must use both hands to hold it.

The sounds grow louder, and the book begins to wriggle. This is madness, but you've got to see what the madness is all about. Taking a deep breath, you pry open the novel.

The world around you spins. The subway station and platform grow dim. The sounds of chirping birds fill your ears. Invisible hands seem to extend from the book's pages and grab you. They pull you into the pages.

And then your world is turned upside down.

Go to the next page.

1

An Outlaw Is Born

It is spring in England, a time when the forests are green and flowers decorate the meadows. The year is 1185, and the country is ruled by King Henry, who sits upon his throne in faraway London. You are a brave youth with a bold heart. Your name is Robin Hood.

News comes to Locksley Town that the Sheriff of Nottingham is holding a shooting match. A grand reward is offered to the archer who shoots best.

You've heard tales of the Sheriff, a cruel man whose guards patrol the land. For years, his troops—members of the King's Guard—have bullied the poor peasants of Locksley. Because of the guards, these poor people must give almost all of their money to the Sheriff.

The Sheriff doesn't scare you, though. When you learn of his contest, you promise victory. You tell your true love, the beautiful Maid Marian, "I'll go, and for you, I'll win."

You gather your bow and arrows, and you start toward Nottingham. As you walk through Sherwood Forest, you think about the prize that you plan to bring home for Maid Marian.

Before long, you come upon a group of fifteen men, foresters, seated beneath a cluster of oak trees. Each wears a dirty tunic the color of dead leaves. Many of them carry bows much larger than your own. You also notice a few swords beside some of the men. The foresters are eating their morning meal.

You duck behind a tree, but it's too late. One of them, a large man, sees you approaching.

"Hello, little lad!" Bits of meat shower his bearded chin. "Where are you off to with such a small bow and a handful of cheap arrows?"

His comments anger you, for you have grown up in a home with little money. You say, "My bow and arrows are as good as yours. I'm on my way to the shooting match at Nottingham. I'll shoot with men twice my age, and I'll win the grand prize."

Another man, this one taller, stands. "Ho!" he says. "Listen to the lad! Barely old enough to walk on his two wobbly legs, and he thinks he can stand among the men at Nottingham."

You boldly say, "I'll bet twenty marks against the best of you that I can hit a target."

For a moment, the foresters are silent. Then they burst into a mighty uproar. Their laughs echo through the treetops, and your cheeks flush with anger.

"Well spoken, young boy," the large forester says.

The tall man towers over you. His voice is low and serious. "There's no target to make good on your wager. Your words are nothing but hot wind."

At the far end of the clearing, your keen eyes spy a herd of deer. They are grazing on grass and berries.

You point to them. "I'll bet twenty marks that I strike down the best among them."

You have shot and killed many animals, but you've never aimed at anything this distant. You wonder if your bow will be strong enough and your aim good enough.

"Done!" cries the large forester, wiping his food-stained chin on his arm. He reaches into his tunic and removes a few crumpled bills. "Here are twenty marks. I'll take your wager."

"Let's see what you're made of, boy," says the tall forester. "And you'd better be able to pay your half of the pledge." His smile is wicked. His breath in your face is hot and sour.

The foresters stand and come forward to watch. The deer remain unaware of the danger. You wonder what you have gotten yourself into.

There is still time to cancel the bet and head toward Nottingham Town. In truth, you only have a few coins in your pockets. So if you take the shot and miss, these men will likely hurt or even kill you. Will you take aim at the deer? Or will you cancel the wager? What will you choose to do?

To shoot at the deer, go to page 71.

To cancel the wager, go to page 78.

"We must get the golden arrow before the contest begins. The question is how?"

The young boy who told you of the traveling party speaks up. "There was another party that passed me. It was a carriage guarded by the King's men."

Little John looks to you. "They could be heading for the western gate of Nottingham. The hidden entrance near the river crossing."

"They wish to enter the city in secret," you say.

"Does the carriage hold our treasure?" asks Will.

"I'm sure of it," you reply. "If we hurry, we can reach the river crossing before that carriage does."

The camp echoes with a mighty, "Huzzah!"

Go to the next page.

You lead the way through the woods, until at last you reach the river. You follow its winding trail west. The Merry Men position themselves about the path, hidden from view.

Soon, you hear the clopping of horse hooves and the squeak of a rusty carriage. The King's men, four in all, guard the carriage on all sides.

As the horsemen approach, you step onto the path. Little John joins you, as does Will.

"Ho there!" you cry.

The guardsmen reach for their blades. "Clear the path," one of them says.

"Not until we relieve you of the treasure you carry. A golden arrow, I presume?"

The guards look to one another suspiciously.

You were correct; the treasure is within your grasp. You step to the carriage boldly and swing open the small, wooden door.

Suddenly, you feel a hot sting of pain as a blade stabs your gut.

From the carriage, a towering man steps out. He wears a horse's hide from head to foot, with a mask to hide his face. In his hand, he holds his sword, which has just cut you deeply.

The man pulls the blade back, and you fall to the ground. "The Sheriff was right to think you'd attack our wagon," he sneers.

Behind you, Little John shouts, "Merry Men, attack!"

A great clamor arises from all sides. But you will not see the outcome of this battle. Your fighting days are done. You close your eyes, picture sweet Marian smiling at you, and breathe your last breath.

Go to page 67.

Backing down from a challenge is not in your nature. If the man wishes you to prove your worth, you shall.

You search the ground for a branch. You find the perfect weapon just twenty yards from the creek. It is straight and six feet in length. You grasp the branch and return to the bridge, trimming away its tender stems.

You glance at the stranger as you ready your staff. He is taller than you by a head and a neck, and he is quite broad across the shoulders.

"Here is my weapon," you say, rapping your new staff against the ground. "Now we shall fight until one of us tumbles into the stream."

The stranger raises his staff and twirls it above his head, between his fingers, until it hums. "Let's have at it then!" he shouts.

You step quickly onto the bridge and deliver a solid blow into the ribs of the stranger. Your strike does little harm; the stranger looks as though you were merely trying to swat a bug.

He returns the blow with one of his own. It is aimed at your head, and you barely have enough time to raise your staff in defense.

You each stand in your place for one good hour. You and the stranger exchange strikes until you are bruised and battered.

At last, you succeed in lashing your adversary with a blow upon the ribs that causes him to totter. He nearly falls off the bridge, but he regains himself quickly.

His sudden recovery stuns you, leaving you open for the hit he lands against the top of your head. Sharp pain stabs at your temples. Your vision blurs and your ears ring.

You blindly swing the staff with all of your might. The stranger wards off the blow. Again he thwacks you, this time in the chest.

You feel yourself falling, and then there is the cool comfort of water. It clears your mind. Climbing to your feet, you trudge to the bank.

"Where are you now, good lad?" shouts the stranger, roaring with laughter. "Care to try once more?"

Your eyes are cloudy, but you catch glimpses of movement around you. You're being surrounded. This battle is only to delay you. The man is keeping you here long enough for his friends to rob you.

Your eyes regain their focus. The movement around you ceases. Are you just being paranoid, or is your life in danger?

Your hand reaches to your side, where the small horn hangs upon a leather strap. The outlaw camp is near. One strong blast of the horn, and your Merry Men will arrive to rescue you. On the other hand, you have been fairly beaten. To call your men will likely get someone hurt. Are you in trouble? Should you call for help? Or will you trust that the stranger is alone and admit that he's won? What will you choose to do?

To admit defeat, go to page 81.

To call for help, go to page 26.

If you turn and stand your ground, you might do something angry and foolish. You choose to remain on the path to Locksley. Your pace quickens, and you glance over your shoulder. The bearded forester strings a second arrow into his bow, so you begin to run.

The tall forester cries out, "Hold your fire, Martin!"

The second shot does not come.

It takes nearly an hour for your nerves to calm and your hands to stop shaking. You stop to rest in the shade of a towering tree. How will you explain this to Marian? What will she think? Will she call you a coward?

A twig snaps nearby, and you scramble to your feet. Once more, you hurry along the path.

Go to the next page.

The sun is at its peak when you reach the village of Locksley. You live near the edge of town, in a small hut. As you arrive, you notice Marian with an armload of clothes to wash.

She nearly drops them when she sees you. "Back so soon?" She smiles. "Was the prize so easily won?"

You drop your gaze as you feel your cheeks redden. "I didn't reach Nottingham. I didn't compete in the match, and I didn't return with anything but shame."

Marian gasps. "Did something happen in Sherwood? Was it the outlaws?"

"I don't wish to speak of it!" You enter the hut and slam the door behind you.

It's not fair to treat Marian this way. She loves you. But your pride has been hurt. So you remain inside.

Later, as the sun sets, you go to chop firewood. You hear the sound of horse hooves. Three riders approach. The two in front wear the armor of the King's Guard. The third is the bearded forester from this morning. A dead deer is slung across the back of his horse. Your arrow is still in the deer's side.

The bearded forester sees you and points the guards in your direction.

"Robin? What's going on?" says Marian, standing beside you now.

You use an arm to keep her back. "Go inside, Marian. Whatever happens, know that I love you."

She does as you ask, closing the door just before the trio of riders reaches your home.

"Are you sure this is the boy?" asks one of the guards. He holds a fiery torch toward you.

The forester nods. His lips curl into a dark sneer of triumph. "The Sheriff of Nottingham will be pleased we found the poacher."

"What's your name, boy?" asks the second guard.

"Robin, sir." Your eyes flicker to the nearby forest. It is close. Were you to run, could you reach it in time?

"In the name of King Henry, you're under arrest for the unlawful hunting of the King's wildlife. Do you admit to this crime?"

You are honorable, and the punishment for lying to a King's Guard is death. You look back to Marian, who peeks at you through a window. "I do," you say.

"Then your fate will be decided by the Sheriff of Nottingham. Come along." The guard places his free hand on the hilt of his sword.

If you go with them, what will the Sheriff do? Will he spare your life? Will he let you go with nothing more than a fine? Or will he put you to death?

On the other hand, you could escape into the forest. But can you reach it before the guards catch you? What will you choose to do?

To go with the guards, go to page 10.

To run for the forest, go to page 64.

You let the man lead you toward the cave. He releases the cool metal from your skin and says, "Quickly."

You get your first good look at him. He is less than ten years older than you, with a scarred face. He puts away the dagger and catches you staring at him. "What are you waiting for? Go."

The cave is low to the ground, and you must crawl to enter it. Inside, it's cool and damp. You strain to see how far back the cave goes, but there is only darkness.

The man follows you into the cave, stopping only for a moment to cover the entrance with a dead branch. He sits by the opening.

"Who are you?" The words escape your lips in a croaking whisper.

The man does not respond. Instead, he places one grimy finger on his lips to silence you. Sure enough, you hear footfalls and the snap of broken twigs. The sounds grow louder as the foresters close in on your hiding place. Before long, they crash past the cave.

You and the stranger remain silent in the cave for a long while. Your muscles ache from crouching, and you are in need of food and water.

Finally, the man removes the branch and steps outside. He scans the woods, then says, "The path is clear, lad. You're safe."

You crawl forward into the sunlight. "Why did you save me?" you ask.

The man shrugs. "I happened upon the foresters just before you, and I saw your whole encounter. You're a fine shot, and you didn't deserve the fate they had planned for you. Besides, outlaws must stick together."

The man extends his hand. "I'm Will Stutely, an outlaw and Merry Man of Sherwood."

You shake his hand. "Robin, formerly of Locksley."

"Come with me, Robin."

Will Stutely leads the way, and it's clear that he knows Sherwood Forest well. You travel south and west, stopping only at the water's edge to drink. The cold water soothes your nerves, allowing you a moment to reflect on all you've lost today. Because of your quick anger, you now must live hidden in the forest for the rest of your life.

Go to the next page.

It's mid-afternoon when Will abandons the path and walks into the depths of Sherwood. You hear voices, laughter, even the soft sound of a harp. Will reaches the top of a slight rise, and you stop beside him.

"There it is," he says.

At the bottom of the hill, in a hidden forest clearing, a small band of men and women feast on cooked meats. Some are gathered around a performer. He is singing and keeping rhythm on a small harp. A number of huts are built along the clearing's edge.

"Who are they?" you ask.

"Others like you," Will answers. "Outlaws and run-aways. Some were caught shooting deer to feed their families. Others were servants who escaped from cruel masters." He looks at you and smiles widely. "Welcome to the Merry Men of Sherwood Forest, Robin Hood!"

2

A Confrontation in Sherwood

In the year that follows, a hundred more men and women join you at your camp. You prove your worth among the outlaws, as an archer and a hunter. You earn a place among their leaders. The Merry Men's vow is simple enough: as the rich stole them from, they will steal back from the rich.

To the poor folk, you give a helping hand. And you return the food and money that has been taken from them. These actions turn you and the Merry Men into heroes of the poor. They whisper your name and tell tales of your good deeds. Soon, the name Robin Hood is known across the land.

The Sheriff of Nottingham and his men search the forest and nearby towns for any sign of you. So far, he has not found your camp, and no Merry Man has fallen into his hands.

You wake one morning in a foul mood. Marian was in your dreams, smiling at you and wishing you a safe return. You miss her more than ever.

The sun has yet to rise, and many still sleep. Those not resting are keeping watch. You fear that the cruel Sheriff will one day find the camp.

You see Will rising from his leafy bed. "Will," you say, "it's been two weeks since we've seen any action."

"Fourteen days of peace and quiet is fine by me," Will answers.

"I've grown restless. I'm going to seek adventure."

"You'll alert us if danger presents itself?" asks Will.

"I will blow three blasts upon my bugle horn, if I need help."

"When we hear it, we'll come quickly," he promises.

You shoulder your bow and a quiver of arrows and stride to the edge of Sherwood Forest. There you wander for a long time.

At last, you take a road back toward camp. The path dips beside a broad, flowing stream. The only way across is a tree-trunk bridge.

As you draw near, you notice a large stranger clad in dusty brown leather. He hurries toward the bridge from the other side. The bridge is too narrow for both of you to cross at the same time. So you quicken your pace, hoping to be the first over. The muscular man does the same. You both step onto the bridge at the same time.

"Stand back," you call out, "and let the better man cross first!"

The man laughs. Beneath his feet, the wooden bridge groans under the strain of his mighty size. "Then stand back, yourself. We both know I'm the better man."

"We'll see," you say, taking the bow and an arrow from your shoulder.

"Only a coward would stand there with a bow to shoot at my heart. I have only a wooden staff."

"I've never thought of myself as a coward. I'll lay down my trusty bow."

"Aye!" the man says. "Then let us fight here on the bridge, until one of us sends the other into the water.

Find a weapon, little one." He leans upon his staff, waiting for you to make a move.

The man is far bigger than you, and your skill with a staff is not great. You also remember the last time you let your anger get out of control; it ended poorly. Should you let the man cross the bridge? Or do you search out a staff and fight him? What will you choose to do?

To let the stranger pass, go to page 68.

To fight the stranger, go to page 49.

You have taken a vow to help those in need. The stranger probably doesn't deserve his punishment. You step forward from the crowd, drawing back your cloak and removing the bow from beneath it. Grabbing an arrow, you string it and take aim at the rope strung between the stranger's wrists.

"Lower your weapon!" The voice comes from behind.

You turn to see two more riders galloping through town. Their sudden arrival dashes any hope of rescuing the stranger.

Two of the nearest guards dismount and approach you. One steals the bow from your hands and crushes it beneath his boot. The other binds your wrists together.

And so, stepping over your broken bow, you begin the long walk to Nottingham. As the guards lead you away, you take comfort in the fact that this kind stranger will be by your side. The thought does not ease your worried mind, though. A lifetime in prison—perhaps even death—are all that await you both.

Go to page 67.

The second guard removes a coil of rope from his saddle. You wait until he's just about to dismount. Then you dash toward the trees.

"Halt!" cries the first guard.

You lower your head and plunge into the dark, thick forest. Branches claw at your arms, hands, and face. When you are safely hidden, you stop and listen.

The guards shout to one another, their voices carrying through the evening air. "After him," the first orders. "If we do not capture him now, he'll return in the night to claim his things."

"Then we must leave him nothing to claim," says the second guard. Without another word, he pulls open the door of your hut. In his hand, he holds a torch.

Marian rushes out, a scream on her lips. She falls to the ground before the guardsman. He tosses the torch through the door.

Smoke begins to plume from the windows. Before long, flames lick the doorframe. Everything you own is going up in flames. It breaks your spirit—and now you fear for Marian's life.

Admitting defeat, you step out from the safety of Sherwood. "I surrender," you say.

The forester laughs at you. One guard readies his weapon. The other ties your hands and Marian's with the rope.

"It's too dark to travel through the forest," says the first guard. "We'll find a place to stay this evening and ride at first light."

"Please," you beg. Your voice sounds cracked and dry. "Marian has done nothing wrong. Release her. I'll put up no fight."

"You should've thought of that before your attempt to escape," says the second guard. He spits at the ground near your feet.

As the guards lead you away, you take comfort in the fact that Marian will be by your side until the very end. The thought does not ease your guilty conscience, though. A lifetime in prison—perhaps even death—are all that await you both.

Go to page 67.

It's a book, and it's making noises. No way are you going to open that!

The sounds grow fainter, and that's cool with you. You scoop the book off the bench. "Ma'am!" you shout.

The woman does not turn. Instead, she joins a small crowd waiting to climb aboard the train.

You run faster, shouting louder. "Ma'am, your book!" You reach her and hold out the heavy book. "You left your book," you say, slightly out of breath.

The woman takes the book and slides it into her bag. "I didn't even know I had this. Thank you." With a smile, she turns and steps onto the subway train.

As you watch the train disappear down the dark tunnel, you wonder what kind of adventure you just missed. It could have been awesome. Life changing.

Oh, well.

You glance at the clock. Still three minutes until your train arrives. With one last glance at the man leaning against the platform's tile wall, you slump onto the bench and wait for your ride home.

Go to the next page.

The End

Try Again

It is adventure you seek today, not a fight. Although it stings your pride a bit, you step off the bridge and bow to the man. "It's too beautiful a day to ruin with fighting," you say.

The stranger nods his head as he crosses toward you. "It was no fight, sir, but all in good fun."

The man lumbers off, leaning from time to time on his staff. He hums a playful tune as he disappears down the western trail.

You cross the bridge, and you spend the rest of the morning hunting. You find no game. As you begin back toward camp, you realize that you have not eaten.

Go to the next page.

You make your way to Hampstead, a nearby village. You raise your hood to hide your face, and you hurry into a tavern that serves grilled meats and vegetables.

It is dark inside and almost empty. You seat yourself in the back and pull a handful of coins from your belt. Before long, a dark-haired woman drops a plate and a mug before you and takes the money without a word.

The food is delicious. But as you break apart a bit of bread, a voice from across the tavern shouts, "Look! A Merry Man of Sherwood!"

You are instantly alert. Your hand goes to the bow at your side. But when you gaze at the elderly man who spoke, you realize that he's not pointing at you. He's gesturing out the tavern's windows.

A small crowd gathers outside. Pulling your hood lower across your face, you rise and join them. Three of the Sheriff's men ride through the village. A captured outlaw, tied to one of their horses, walks behind.

"It cannot be a Merry Man," says an old woman. "They wear green. Do they not?"

"Yes," you say, straining to see the captive. "They certainly do."

As one of the guards passes, you recognize their prisoner. It is the towering gentleman from the bridge.

You feel an urge to help the stranger. With your bow, you could shoot through the rope and free him. But is it wise? You don't know the man. He could be a murderer. On the other hand, he might be a kind fellow getting led to his doom. Should you try to save him? Or is it wiser to do nothing? What will you choose to do?

To rescue the stranger, go to page 63.

To do nothing, go to page 34.

The men close in on you, blocking your path. You've never shot an animal at such a distance, but that doesn't mean you can't.

You tighten your grip on the bow and slide an arrow into place. You raise the bow. Your hands shake. A nervous breath escapes your lips as you draw the feather of the arrow to your ear. You aim for the largest deer in the herd. And you release the arrow.

The bowstring rings, and the shot speeds away. The deer leaps high into the air as the arrow pierces its side. Your aim is true. The deer falls dead.

The men say nothing. One of them dashes across the glade to inspect your shot.

"How do you like that?" you say to the heavyset man whose jaw hangs open. "I'll take my winnings."

The bearded forester slams his fist down on a dry log. It splinters from the blow. "No!" he cries. His dirty hand clutches the marks. He shoves the money back into his tunic. "Be gone, boy!"

You do not move. The twenty marks are a great prize. With them, you can purchase a fine gift for Marian. "I won't leave without my winnings," you reply. "Besides, my kill should feed you well for days. Twenty marks is a small price to pay."

The large forester's jaw clenches shut in rage, and he speaks through his teeth. "Boy, I'll make it so you never draw a bow again."

The tall figure beside you adds, "It was a foolish play. The deer of Sherwood are the King's animals. By the law, your action should be reported to the Sheriff."

Your stomach twists into a knot. You shoulder your bow and quickly retreat toward the path.

"Catch him!" one of the foresters shouts.

"No," says another. "Let him go. He's just a boy."

"And what of the reward?" asks the heavyset man. "King Henry would favor knowledge of the boy's deed. Who knows how many marks the boy would get us?"

"He's not worth it," the tall man says.

You stride away from them, down the forest path. You have forgotten the shooting match and wish only to return home in peace.

You reach the trees along the path to Locksley when the large forester shouts, "Flee!" He grabs his bow and fits an arrow into it. "Let me hurry you along, foolish boy!" He sends the arrow whistling toward you.

The wind beside your left ear splits, as his shot passes three inches from your head. Whether he missed on purpose or not, you don't care. Your life is in danger.

You could stand your ground and prove your bravery to this band of foresters. Or you could hurry on the path home. But which is the wiser option? What will you choose to do?

To stand your ground, go to page 32.

To continue home, go to page 52.

It takes all of your will power to turn your back on Maid Marian. You love her dearly, but going to her could be a grave mistake. So you step inside the striped tent to take your place among the archers.

They are gathered in groups of two and three. Some talk loudly of the great shots they've made. Others study their bows to see that their weapons are ready. You spot the Sheriff's own archer, the famed Gill of the Red Cap. He inspects an arrow to make sure it will fly straight. You have never seen a company of men like this before. England's best archers have all come to Nottingham.

Go to the next page.

From outside, the sound of many bugles blares. Men hurry through the tent flaps, back onto the range. You follow and discover that the Sheriff of Nottingham has arrived. He rides upon a beautiful white horse. The Sheriff wears a purple robe and cap, with a golden chain hanging from his neck. His lady sits upon a brown horse beside him. She is dressed in blue velvet.

The crowd claps as the Sheriff and his lady dismount. Two guards with spears flank them. A third man stands behind the Sheriff. This guard stands out from the rest. He is clad in a horse's hide, with a mask that covers his face. A heavy sword hangs from his waist.

"That's Guy of Gisbourne," says the archer beside you. "He's the Sheriff's private guard."

When the Sheriff is seated, an announcer sounds three blasts from his silver horn. The archers all step forward, you among them, while the announcer reads the rules of the game.

"Each archer is to shoot one arrow. The ten who shoot the best will be chosen to fire again. From these, the finest three shall be asked to shoot. He who lets fly the best arrow shall be given the prize!"

The archers shoot, each man in turn. The crowd cheers and calls out the name of their favorite bowman. When the first round is nearly complete, six arrows have struck the target: four outside its black ring, two within.

It is your turn to shoot. All eyes are upon you as you step to the line. The crowd is silent, waiting as you aim—and fire. The arrow soars. It strikes the target near the center, and the crowd cheers with delight.

"A fine shot," the man beside you says.

"Fine enough, I suppose."

And so ten men are left. Six of them are famous throughout the land. But to the Sheriff and the crowd, you are just a man known as Jack of Teviotdale.

As the men prepare for their next shot, you notice the Sheriff studying the archers. He is searching for you, for Robin Hood. Your disguise hides your identity well, though. The Sheriff does not give Jack of Teviotdale a second glance.

"You're a fine shot, boy," says a man behind you.

Your stomach becomes a cold pit as you recognize the voice. It is the tall forester whom you encountered in the forest last year.

The forester stands with the other remaining archers. One hand is on his hip, the other on his bow.

If the forester sees through your disguise, he does not say so. Instead, he says, "Shall we wager on your next shot? Does twenty marks sound like a fair bet?"

The forester has you in a tough spot. If you ignore him, he may become suspicious. He could alert the Sheriff about you. But if you speak with him, he might discover your secret. What will you choose to do?

To ignore the forester, go to page 24.

To speak with the forester, go to page 14.

Even from this distance, you feel strongly that you can shoot a deer. Yet if you miss, you'll need to pay, and you don't have enough money.

The men close in on you, blocking your path toward Locksley. You grip the bow tightly but do not raise it.

"What are you waiting for?" asks the large man.

You step backward and shake your head. "I'm sorry, kind men. I changed my mind. If you do not mind, I'll be on my way."

"What are you, a coward?" The words escape the forester's lips like venom.

It takes all of your willpower not to speak out against him. Instead, you spin on your heels and stride toward Nottingham and its shooting match.

You step along the rocky path, but the heavyset man shouts, "Boy!"

You turn and see that he has grabbed his bow and fitted an arrow into it. "Let me hurry you along to your match then, foolish boy!" He lets the arrow fly. His shot passes no more than three inches from your head.

You dash away. The thought of an arrow striking you draws you off the path and into the maze of trees.

"Run, coward!" you hear the large forester shout. His words echo through the glade.

You rush on for more than an hour, trying to stay as close to the path as possible. Low-hanging branches tear at your face and arms.

At last, when you are certain the strangers are no longer a threat, you climb up a tall tree. You search for the path but do not find it.

Panic begins to fill your heart. Sherwood Forest is not familiar to you, and you are terribly lost. You recall tales of outlaws who live in the woods, helping those in need. You cry out for guidance, hoping these mythical figures might help you.

Not sure what else to do, you climb down a steep crag of rocks. But the stone beneath you gives out. You begin to slide. Your left foot wedges between two sharp stones, and you hear bones snap. Pain wraps its way up your leg and takes the breath from you.

You fall forward, and your forehead crashes against a blunt stone. Your foot comes loose, and you slide onto a bed of moss. You realize with dread that this will be your final resting place.

Your vision begins to swim, and you feel the strength leaving you. You close your eyes, imagining the lovely Marian smiling down on you. The pain fades, and you welcome the eternal sleep.

Go to page 67.

The stranger has beaten you, and you are just being paranoid. You realize the silliness of your worries, and you can no longer stop yourself from laughing. The stranger relaxes his grip on his weapon and crosses the bridge. It creaks and bends under his weight.

When he reaches your side, he helps you to your feet. "You're a brave and noble lad," he says.

"You're a worthy opponent," you say.

You remove the horn from your belt and toot a single blast that echoes through the forest. Before long, your Merry Men arrive, led by Will Stutely.

Will asks, "Why are you wet from head to foot?"

You nod at the stranger. "This fellow gave me a good drubbing, and I took a tumble into the water."

Will advances on the stranger. "Then he shall receive a drubbing, as well!"

"Halt," you snap. "Leave him be. He's a good man."

The men—about to leap upon the stranger—stop at the sound of your voice.

"Who are you people?" the stranger asks.

"We're outlaws, a band known as the Merry Men of Sherwood. I'm Robin Hood."

The man's eyes widen. "Robin Hood? The Sheriff offers a reward for your capture. Had I known your name before, I might have claimed the Sheriff's reward."

"What's to stop you now?"

The man nods at the outlaws surrounding him. "A band of armed men," he laughs.

You like this stranger. His size and strength would make a welcome addition to the Merry Men.

"Would you like to join us?" you ask. "We could use a strong fellow such as you."

The man considers your offer. "Are the tales true? Do you steal from the wealthy to give to the poor?"

"We do."

"Then I shall gladly join."

You clap the stranger's shoulder. "We've gained a good man today. What name do you go by?"

"I'm John Little."

Will, who enjoys a good laugh, speaks up. "Oh yes, little you are indeed."

Go to page 37.

You don't trust any man who would hold a dagger to your throat. Before he can drag you into the cave, you drive your heel onto his foot. You elbow him in the stomach and break free of his grasp.

"Fool," he hisses through gritted teeth.

You run with all of your might down the winding path. Suddenly, you feel a sharp and immediate pain between your shoulder blades. An arrow has struck you, causing you to stumble. But you do not fall.

A second arrow finds its mark in your left leg, and it drives you onto one knee. You turn your head and see the foresters advancing. One of the men strings an arrow, draws it back, and releases it. It speeds through the air, straight toward you. Then everything is black.

Go to page 67.

The Sheriff waits for your answer, and a hush falls across the crowd. You bow your head and say, "Many thanks, but I must decline your offer. Sadly, my brother is ill. Seeing the prize will lift his spirit."

The Sheriff's lip curls into a frown. "Very well, Jack of Teviotdale. I'm disappointed by your choice, but it is yours to make. Here is your prize."

He hands you the golden arrow, which you take with both hands. Its worth will feed many who lack food. This thought pleases you.

You drop to one knee. "My Lord, I'm honored."

The announcer cries, "Hurray for Jack of Teviotdale!"

The audience shouts its pleasure again.

As you leave, you hear the Sheriff speaking to his trusted guard. "It's a disappointment," he says. "The coward Robin Hood dared not come today."

You don't hear Guy of Gisbourne's response, for you must depart quickly. Weaving through the crowd is difficult. Men and women offer their congratulations. They clap you on the shoulder and ask to see the prize. You spy Little John leaning against the wall of the city gate. And then you hear a familiar voice.

"Master Teviotdale?"

It's Marian. She sounds nervous.

It tears at your heart, leaving her like this. But escape is your main concern. You continue onward.

"Master Teviotdale," Marian calls your name again. Her voice is nearly a shout.

Two of the King's Guard notice the commotion. One rests his hand on the hilt of a sword.

"Robin, is it you?"

Her voice continues to get louder. If you don't reply, Marian might accidentally reveal your identity to the guards. Yet, if you stop for a moment, you might be giving the guards extra time to catch you. Should you ignore Marian and hurry your escape? Or should you talk to her? What will you choose to do?

To ignore Maid Marian, go to page 122.

To speak with her, go to page 132.

You pull back on the reins, bringing the horse to a stop in the middle of the road. "Ho," you say, steadying the tired steed.

It chuffs and shakes its head. You quickly dismount and tie the horse to a nearby tree.

"I'll find us something to drink," you promise.

You notice a small field beside the road and hope that there's a farm or village nearby. You trek across the field and soon arrive at a farmhouse. There, you meet an elderly woman.

"Hello!" you call to her.

The woman does not seem alarmed. Instead, she nods and says, "Good day to you."

"I wonder if I could trouble you for some water. My horse is in need of a drink."

The woman waddles to her barn and returns with a wooden bucket full of water. She drops the bucket at your feet and says, "Fresh from our well."

"Thank you," you say with gratitude.

You carry the full, sloshing bucket across the field to your waiting horse. It drinks the water eagerly.

For four days you ride, resting only a few hours each night. At last, you pass into Sherwood Forest. By the time you reach the edge of camp, Little John and Will are waiting for you.

"You come empty-handed?" Little John teases. "I expected a stack of gifts from the King."

You aren't in a joking mood. After dismounting, you explain the Sheriff's plot.

"What will you have us do?" asks Little John.

"Prepare the camp for the Sheriff's attack. Each man shall be armed at all times. The Sheriff will use Marian to find us. And when he does find us, we'll be ready."

Go to the next page.

For seven long days, you remain in camp. Finally, on the eighth day, you see one of your men—David of Doncaster—walking along the path toward you. He is not alone; a woman walks beside him.

"Marian!" you exclaim.

You dash toward her, and when she sees you, her eyes grow wide. You hug Marian tightly, as she cries against your chest.

"I found her at the Blue Boar," David says. "She was looking for you." He bows and then leaves the two of you alone.

You whisper into Marian's ear. "What is it, Marian? What's wrong?"

Marian begins to mumble. At first, you cannot make out the words. But then you hear, "I'm sorry, Robin. I'm so sorry. You must forgive me."

You lean close to her ear and whisper, "I know."

Suddenly, the forest is alive with soldiers, far more than you ever expected. Armed against you with bows, swords, and axes, they smash through the underbrush and surround the camp. At their lead is the Sheriff, whose madness shows in his unruly hair and wild eyes.

"Here it is!" the Sheriff cheers. "The home of Robin Hood and his Merry Men!"

You are dangerously outnumbered, but you shield Marian with your body. The Sheriff has you, and he knows it. If only you had more men!

With a wicked laugh, the Sheriff raises his hand, and his men ready their weapons. Many of them point in your direction.

"Stay behind me," you say to Marian.

"Until my dying breath," she answers.

"Attack!" the Sheriff commands.

His men cheer as they crash into the camp. You close your eyes as the Sheriff's bowmen release their shots. Fortunately, you barely have time to feel pain as the arrows hit their target.

Go to page 67.

You've dedicated your life to helping those in need. And there are none in greater need than the child. As you pull your hood low, a fresh set of hooves thunders from behind Will's cart. It is Guy of Gisbourne, in his frightening armor of metal and horsehide. His sword is drawn for battle.

"What is the cause of our delay?" Guy calls out. He stops his horse beside Will's cart.

You push forward, through the crowd, hanging your head low. As you reach the crying child and grab his arm, you say, "Apologies, my lord."

"I should arrest you both," the Sheriff snaps, before nudging his horse forward once more.

You carry the boy to a nearby storefront and carefully set him down. You use a sleeve to dry his eyes and clear the dirt from his face. "Are you hurt?" you ask.

The boy shakes his head but says nothing.

You hand him an apple. "Be careful where you walk." You ruffle his hair, then place a coin from your belt into the shopkeeper's hand.

By the time you make your way back through the crowd, the army is almost to the edge of town. There, a small wooden stage awaits. This is where Will is to be executed. You wish you could alert your friend to your presence. But he keeps his head low until the cart comes to a stop.

One of the guards dismounts and pulls Will from the cart. A crowd of onlookers gathers around the stage on all sides, as the guard leads Will up the wooden steps.

Go to the next page.

Little John finds his way to your side, and you know that it's time to attack. Yet when you reach for your bow, Little John stops you.

"No, I will do it," he says.

"I'm to blame for Will's capture," you respond. "So I'll be the one to lead this charge."

Little John shakes his head. "No, Robin, it will be better if I take the lead. You're best used as our second line of defense."

You must do something. If you don't, your friend will die. But should you step forward? Or will you let Little John lead the way? What will you choose to do?

To lead the rescue, go to page 109.

To let Little John lead, go to page 116.

The Sheriff waits for your answer, and a hush falls over the crowd. You wish to flee with your prize, but you don't dare to decline such an offer. You drop to one knee and bow your head. "It would please me greatly to join you for dinner."

The Sheriff presents you with the golden arrow, which you take with both hands. Its worth will feed many who lack food. This thought pleases you.

The announcer cries, "Behold! Jack of Teviotdale!"

The audience shouts its pleasure once more.

As you stand, the Sheriff claps you on the shoulder. "Come. Let's feast."

Go to the next page.

You're escorted through the excited crowd and into a looming castle. Leading the way is the frightening guard known as Guy of Gisbourne. You follow him up a long, winding stone stairway lined with torches. At the top of the stairs is a wide room. Inside, you see a large oak table filled with food: roasted meats, fresh vegetables and fruits, baskets of cooked breads, and more. Your stomach rumbles at the sight.

The Sheriff sits in a cushioned chair at one end of the table. His lady sits at the far end. In the middle, a third chair is placed. The nearest guard nods, and you sit.

You eat in silence; soon the amount of food begins to anger you. There are far too many who are poor and hungry, while the Sheriff feasts like this every day!

A guard enters the dining hall, and you try to ignore him. But when you see him whisper to the Sheriff, you begin to worry. The Sheriff looks at you for a moment. His gaze becomes a glare. Then he gestures to the guard whom you didn't know was behind you.

The guard draws back a club and swings. It connects solidly behind your right ear. Pain erupts in your head, washing over you. And then the world goes black.

You wake to see the cold, stone walls and metal bars of a prison cell. You shake your head to clear it. Your tongue feels like sandpaper against your lips.

A man lurks in the shadows of the hall outside. You strain to see him better, and he steps into the nearby light from a window. It's the Sheriff of Nottingham.

A black cloak is pulled tightly across his armored chest. His gray eyes stare at you. "The famed Robin Hood," he says. "Your disguise might have worked, if my guards hadn't caught three of your Merry Men waiting for you." He laughs cruelly. "Now, you are mine forever! Enjoy your stay, Robin Hood." With that, the Sheriff turns and stalks away.

The small window in your cell offers just a sliver of light. It shines weakly against your face. The walls of the cell suddenly feel like a coffin. It's hard to breathe.

You fall onto the floor, your back resting against the metal bars. This is how your life will end. Sitting here. In the dark. Alone.

Go to page 67.

You have waited long enough. One way or another, this battle with the Sheriff must end today.

You speak in a low voice to Marian. "When I make my move, find a place to hide until the battle is over." Then, raising the sword over your head, you shout, "Merry Men, King's Guard, attack!"

Arrows whistle through the air in every direction. You charge forward, swinging your blade at Guy of Gisbourne. Beside you, Little John engages the Sheriff.

Up and down you fight. The grass is crushed beneath your heels. The ground around you is sprinkled with bright red drops. Men from both sides fall, but you and Guy of Gisbourne remain locked in combat.

Your opponent makes a fierce thrust. You leap back but trip on a root; you fall heavily onto your back. Guy of Gisbourne leaps at you, a grin of rage upon his face. He stabs with his sword. You swipe with your hand. The blade cuts your palm, but you bat the point away. The sword plunges deep into the ground beside you.

Standing quickly, you snatch your sword. Panic fills Guy of Gisbourne's gray eyes. Seeing that he is unarmed, you step forward and throw a punch.

Guy of Gisbourne falls to the hard-packed earth, and you raise your blade to his throat. He closes his eyes and awaits your final blow.

Instead, you drop the sword to your side and speak. "Do you surrender?"

Guy of Gisbourne croaks, "Yes, I surrender."

"Then I see no reason to harm you further."

And so the battle ends.

You turn to see Little John standing before the unconscious Sheriff. David of Doncaster wraps thick coils of rope around the Sheriff's wrists. When he finishes, he does the same to Guy of Gisbourne and the rest of the Sheriff's men.

The prisoners are all tied to the trunks of great oak trees, where they spend the night under constant watch by members of the King's Guard. You mourn your lost men in silence, with Marian at your side. Your muscles ache; the battle has sapped your strength. Before long, you find yourself drifting to sleep.

Go to the next page.

Early the next morning, you begin your trip back to London. Marian rides behind you in the saddle. The Merry Men join you as well, leaving the camp behind in order to train with the King's Guard.

You cause a stir as you pass through Nottingham. Cheers erupt in the streets. Cries of "Robin Hood! Robin Hood!" echo throughout the town.

In that moment, you make a silent vow. You will continue to do whatever you can to ensure that no man, woman, or child will ever go hungry again.

Go to page 150.

The child is in need, but you won't get a better chance to free your friend than this. You turn to Little John and say, "Help the boy, and keep the guards' attention."

Little John speeds away, pressing through the crowd, toward the child.

As you cross to the wooden cart, you remove a small dagger from your belt. Will's tired eyes look up as you approach, and relief floods through them. But the relief turns instantly to horror.

"Robin," he cries out, "beware!"

Turning around, you see the terrible guard dressed in horse hide, the one called Guy of Gisbourne. His blade is drawn, and he swings his sword in a mighty slash.

The pain is intense as the blade rips across your chest. You gasp for breath as you fall to your knees, collapse, and then roll onto your back. You press your hands to your chest, feeling the life drain from you.

A horse draws near you, and you see the Sheriff of Nottingham. A twisted smile parts his lips as you are swallowed by eternal darkness.

Go to page 67.

You will not be the first to strike. You'll wait to see what your enemy chooses to do. And so you grip your sword tightly, watching every move that the Sheriff and Guy of Gisbourne make.

"We've come all this way, Robin. Do you intend to fight?" The Sheriff's venomous words send spit shooting from his cracked lips.

You speak in a low voice to Marian. "When I make my move, find a place to hide until this battle is over."

As you return your gaze to the Sheriff, you spy one of his men—a young lad barely old enough to carry a weapon. The boy has an arrow aimed in your direction, but the bow in his hands shakes. His arm is not strong enough to hold the arrow back.

An accidental shot is fired. The boy's arrow cuts through the air, leaving you only a moment to twist out of the way. The sharp tip slices your sleeve, scratching you but doing no real damage.

At least, that's what you think, until you hear her voice. "Robin?" The word is a short gasp in your ear, almost a whisper.

Your stomach tightens as you face Marian again. She stands, arms stretched toward you. The arrow has struck near her heart.

She begins to fall, and you swiftly drop your sword to catch her. Lowering her to the ground, you cradle her. Tears begin to well in your eyes, blurring your vision.

You place Marian's head gently on the earth, and you are suddenly filled with anger. You pick up your weapon, and cry, "Merry Men, King's Guard, attack!"

With a roar of outrage, you advance on Guy of Gisbourne. Your strikes at him are fast but careless. He easily deflects them. With one mighty swing, you lose your balance and turn sideways to your opponent.

He seizes the opportunity. His sword pierces your side. You drop your weapon and clutch the wound.

You stagger across the battlefield to where Marian lies unmoving. You fall beside her and close your eyes. There, the peace of eternal sleep finds you.

Go to page 67.

Just four men leading one wagon? Even if this is a trap, there are more than enough Merry Men with you to handle it. Besides, with winter nearing, you'll need all of the supplies you can get. And so you slide the bow off your shoulder and step lightly from the underbrush.

"Robin," Little John hisses.

"Calm yourself, friend," you reply.

As you block the road, the riders bring their horses to a halt. Little John and Will Stutely join you.

"What is this?" asks the first rider.

"Greetings! I am Robin Hood, and these are my Merry Men of Sherwood. Now, kindly give us your wagon of goods, and be on your way."

"I think not, bandit." The lead rider draws back his woolen cloak. Beneath, he wears the armor of the King's Guard. A sword hangs at his side.

The other riders follow suit.

"A trap?" you mutter.

Little John grunts in response.

The first rider gallops forward, his sword in hand. To your surprise, six more guards pour out from the wagon. You've been ambushed and now stand outnumbered.

You quickly kneel, dodging a guard's mighty swing. Stringing an arrow into your bow, you fire upon the guard. The arrow strikes his armor, leaving him stunned but not hurt.

Suddenly, you feel a blade slice across your back. The bow falls from your hand, and you drop to your knees.

"Robin!" Little John's cry echoes through the forest.

You feel the strength draining from your body as the guard readies his blade for another swing.

You close your eyes just before the coming attack. And then there is nothing.

Go to page 67.

Curiosity once again gets the better of you. As dangerous as it may be, you'll go to London. You bow your head and respond, "I'll do our King's bidding."

You pack a bag and dress for the journey, choosing to disguise yourself in blue. Beneath your costume, you wear a coat of linked mail; it's strong enough that no arrow can pierce it.

The messenger is blindfolded again and put on his horse, while you say your farewells. It'll be a long journey to London, and as you ride away from camp, you cannot help but wonder if you'll ever see your friends again.

For four days and nights, you travel along twisted paths and through villages and forests. At last, you arrive at the walls of famous London. If a trap awaits, the King has yet to spring it.

Dismounting, you leave your horse in a small stable. You pass several guards as you make your way into the castle, and they nod their heads at you. You walk through stone hallways, up a winding staircase, and into the King's Throne Room. Your footsteps echo across the vast, open room.

King Richard sits upon the throne. Sunshine pours in, dancing off his armor and jeweled crown. Even seated, King Richard is a strong figure with silver hair and a great beard. Because of his bravery, he is known by many as Richard the Lionheart, and it seems like a fitting title.

You kneel, saying, "King Richard, I give myself as your servant and will do as you command."

"Rise, Robin Hood," the King booms.

Upon standing, you feel a bit nervous, wondering why the King has asked you to come.

"You've been quite a problem," the King says. "You live in my woods, pay me no taxes, and steal from my wealthy citizens. I'm surprised my father, King Henry, allowed such behavior."

Your chest tightens as you say, "My apologies, Your Majesty."

"At least there's kindness in your intentions. Your peace and good standing among the people is not lost on me." A hint of a smile plays upon King Richard's lips. He stands. "King Henry had a fool leading his men."

"The Sheriff of Nottingham," you say.

"Indeed." The King paces with his hands behind his back. "Do you not wonder why I've brought you here, outlaw?"

You nod and say, "I do."

"Three days ago, my men heard of a plot by the old Sheriff and his man, Guy of Gisbourne. They intend to find your camp by striking Sherwood. They're prepared to burn the forest to the ground if they must."

"How does he plan to find me?"

"He has a woman, a maiden from Locksley."

"Marian?" you blurt. Your stomach turns to stone. How has the Sheriff discovered your true love?

"I offer you a deal, Robin Hood. My army needs brave men, and I need to clear the forest of outlaws. Become a member of the King's Guard. Stand at my side, and you and your men will be forgiven. You'll also have my help in stopping the Sheriff, once and for all."

Go to the next page.

Your mind races, and it's hard to think. You've lived happy and free for so long. Are you willing to give that life up—to live at the command of another? Or are you better off returning to Sherwood and fighting the Sheriff your own way, however you think is best? Will you accept the King's offer or hurry back to Sherwood? What will you choose to do?

To accept the King's offer, go to page 146.

To return to Sherwood, go to page 114.

You don't stand a chance against a skilled fighter such as Guy of Gisbourne. To challenge him with a sword would mean almost certain death. If there's a chance to save Will, it's with a bow in your hands.

Guy of Gisbourne snarls and leaps upon you. You quickly drop to one knee, string an arrow in your bow, and fire. Your aim is true, and the arrow slices him across his right elbow. He roars, dropping his arm but not releasing the blade. To your surprise, he shakes off the wound and raises the sword again.

You scramble for another arrow, string it with speed, and release it. This time, it strikes Guy of Gisbourne in the chest, shattering against his armor plate. The arrow doesn't even faze him. Guy of Gisbourne speeds forward and swings his sword before you can fire a third time.

A sharp pain burns your stomach. You gasp for breath but do not find it. You've been defeated because you chose poorly. It's the last thought you have before the blackness overtakes you forever.

Go to page 67.

"This task is mine," you say to Little John. Before your trusted friend can protest further, you draw back your cloak and remove your bow. Then you reach into the quiver, grab an arrow, and string it. Closing one eye and exhaling slowly, you aim at the rope above Will's neck, and you fire. The arrow slices through the air, cutting the rope.

The crowd gasps. The Sheriff's guards draw their swords. You quickly aim a second arrow at the Sheriff.

"Allow his freedom," you say. "Or I'll shoot again."

"You're a fool, Robin Hood," the Sheriff says. "Do you think I wouldn't prepare my men for you?" And then he laughs, a roaring sound that chills your bones.

You suddenly feel an arrow pierce your back. The pain spreads through your body, and you drop your bow. You spin around and glance at a nearby tower. Standing inside the tower, with a bow in hand, is one of the Sheriff's guards.

You drop to one knee and curse your sloppy mistake. They are the last words that escape your dying lips.

Go to page 67.

You crouch back under the cover of trees. As the wagon passes, you spot something hidden beneath one of the rider's cloaks: a sword. This is no simple wagon of goods. It's a trap. Little John was right.

You wait until the wagon is long past, and then you continue toward camp. You arrive at midday, and you immediately gather your Merry Men.

"We must be careful," you say. "The Sheriff has set traps for us. We will not do battle, but we must hide silently in Sherwood so that everyone may be well."

One of your men, Allan of Dale, speaks up. "What if we are forced to defend ourselves?"

"Then use your weapons with might," you respond. "Let's hope, though, that it won't come to that."

Weeks go by, and you remain hidden. You ignore the wealthy travelers that pass along the Great North Road. Instead, you prepare the camp for winter by drying meats and repairing the roofs of many huts.

The Sheriff's men are never seen by any of your scouts. You begin to wonder if they've given up the hunt. You grow restless, and early one morning you decide to visit the Blue Boar. Perhaps Eadom has some news to share.

You gather your bow and arrows, a pouch of dried meat, and your horn. You put on a cloak to hide your weapons, and you begin on your way. Will Stutely is chopping firewood at the edge of camp. You tell him your intentions.

He wipes sweat from his brow and says, "It's foolish to go alone, Robin."

"It's a simple trek. I'll be back before midday."

Will drives his axe into a stump. "I'll go with you." He hurries to his resting area to grab a few supplies. When he returns, he is clad in a long cloak and armed with a sword.

With your companion at your side, you begin on your way.

Go to the next page.

When you come to the edge of the forest, you see two bands of the Sheriff's men. You pull your hood close to your face and fold your hands as if in prayer. Will does the same, and the guards ignore you—if they see you at all.

The rest of your trip passes without incident, and at last you come to the Blue Boar. You enter and sit at a distant bench.

As you wait for Eadom, the tavern door opens and in walks a deputy with three of the King's Guard. Your heartbeat quickens as the deputy and his men sit at a table near you. At first, they don't notice you. But soon the deputy glances your way.

"You there!" he demands. "Why do you wear woolen robes on such a warm autumn day?"

Will responds, "We go to Canterbury Town."

"That doesn't answer my question," the deputy snaps. "And I can't help but notice you wear green beneath your robes. It makes me think that perhaps you're members of Robin Hood's Merry Men!"

You quickly make eye contact with Eadom, and you see recognition on his face. He strides over to the deputy and places himself between you and the King's Guard. "Is there trouble, my Lord?" he says.

Will leans to you and whispers, "Your arrows aren't much good in here. You must go. I'll hold them off with my sword for as long as I can."

"I cannot leave you here," you reply sharply.

"We must separate. You're far too valuable to be captured. You can escape out the tavern's back door."

You hear shouting outside the tavern as more of the King's Guard arrive on horseback. The time to act is now. Should you stay and fight with Will? Or will you escape alone through the back door? What will you choose to do?

To stay and fight, go to page 138.

To escape, go to page 143.

Whatever the King may offer, you cannot give up your life in Sherwood. You will not allow yourself to be in debt to him or his kingdom.

"What do you say, Robin?" King Richard asks.

You bow. "My apologies, but I must say no."

"And be an outlaw for life?" the King snaps.

"I care only for Marian."

"If you refuse, then we must become enemies," the King declares.

"I'm truly sorry." With these words, you turn and run as fast as your legs will take you. Out of the throne room. Down the winding steps. Through the castle halls. And to the stable.

You find your horse and quickly spur it to action. The ride is four days, and you haven't any time to spare.

Go to the next page.

You ride, day and night, until your horse pants for breath. You continue to gallop as fast as the horse can carry you. But eventually your mount grows tired, and you fear it will not last much longer. Should you stop now, alone and in the middle of nowhere? Or should you press on to the next village, where food and drink can be had? What will you choose to do?

To rest now, go to page 86.

To keep riding, go to page 131.

Little John looks to you, and you nod. He moves quickly, pushing between the guards in an attempt to reach the stage.

One of the riders dismounts and draws his sword. "Halt!" he orders.

Little John swings his staff and clobbers the guard's helmet. The guard drops to his knees, dazed, but John does not stop. With long strides, he stalks toward the stage, until he stands before the Sheriff's horse.

The Sheriff smirks. "A Merry Man? You'll die for showing yourself here."

From the corner of your eye, you spy a glint of metal. Gazing upward, you notice a guard tower. A soldier there is stringing an arrow into his bow and taking aim at Little John.

You shed your cloak and draw an arrow of your own. You string it, aim, and fire. Your shot speeds above the crowd, striking the archer's bow before he can let his arrow fly. The archer drops his bow, and it twists end over end to the ground.

The crowd gasps in surprise.

"Robin Hood!" shouts the Sheriff.

He spurs his horse as he swings his blade downward. John ducks under the horse's belly, and the Sheriff's blow whistles harmlessly over his head.

The Sheriff spins toward the stage and yells to the guards there. "Get on with it! Kill the prisoner!"

Prompted into motion, the guards string a rope around Will's neck. At the same moment, you take the horn from your belt and blow it three times. From all around the crowd, Merry Men draw their weapons and attack the Sheriff's men.

Steel clashes against steel as the Merry Men wage war against the King's Guard. Swords flash and arrows whistle through the air.

"They're everywhere!" howls the Sheriff. "Retreat!" He turns his horse and gallops away.

You send an arrow past him as you shout, "You call Robin Hood a coward? You're the coward, Sheriff!"

Many of the guards follow him away, but many others remain locked in battle with the Merry Men. As you spin around to look for an opponent, you find Guy of Gisbourne before you. His armor chimes and creaks as he steps forward.

"Greetings, archer," he says with a confident smirk.

You quickly arm your bow and hold it before you.

"Your arrows may have scared away the Sheriff, but they won't have the same effect on me." Guy of Gisbourne pulls an abandoned sword from the ground and tosses it at your feet. "Pick up the sword, and face me like a man," he demands.

Will you go blade against blade with the skilled Guy of Gisbourne? Or will you fire at him with your bow? What will you choose to do?

To grab the sword, go to page 140.

To fire your bow, go to page 108.

6

The New King

Winter blankets the earth in snow. You remain in camp most days. Occasionally, you trudge to the Blue Boar for a warm meal. There is no news of the Sheriff. He has fled from power, humiliated by his cowardice. This news relieves you. Guy of Gisbourne, too, is nowhere to be found. This news does not relieve you.

The land of England is ripe with change this season. King Henry has died, and King Richard now wears the crown. You admire the new king. He is brave and has been through adventures as exciting as your own.

Many long, cold months pass. Eventually, the buds of spring appear, and the snow is replaced by green. The camp resumes its practices of hunting and feasting.

On a spring morning, fresh and bright, you awaken to birds singing. Little John and Friar Tuck hum happy tunes. You sit down to eat a quick breakfast, when there comes the sound of a horse's hooves.

You turn to find Will hurrying down the forest path, leading a milk-white horse. Atop the horse sits a messenger of the King—a boy no more than sixteen years old. His long, yellow hair flows behind him as he rides, and he wears jewels that flash in the sunlight. The boy's eyes are covered by a blindfold to hide the location of your secret camp.

Will says, "I discovered this boy at the Blue Boar. He was speaking with Eadom about you, Robin."

You stand. "A messenger of the King? In Sherwood?"

The messenger blindly searches for you. "I come on behalf of our lord, King Richard."

"You're a long way from the castle in London," you say. "Have you taken a wrong turn?"

Will helps the boy off his horse and removes the dark blindfold.

Upon seeing you, the messenger says, "I come with greetings from our noble King. He has heard of your merry doings, and it would please him greatly to meet you in person."

"King Richard asks for me?" You can hardly believe the boy's words.

"Yes," the boy answers simply.

You're not sure what to think about this news. While King Richard is not your enemy, you are an outlaw. Living here, in Sherwood, you're in direct opposition to the King. You hunt and feast upon wildlife that only he is legally allowed to hunt. Does the King have noble intentions? Or is this a trap? The messenger awaits your answer. Will you go with him or not? What will you choose to do?

To travel to London, go to page 104.

To remain in Sherwood, go to page 128.

It goes against your hopes and wishes to leave Marian behind, but you must. You lower your head and proceed toward the gates. Marian continues to plead and begins to follow you.

One of the guards steps in front of you and blocks your path. "What's the lady want?" he barks.

You try to remain calm. "It's been a tiring day. I'd like to leave in peace."

The second guard moves behind you. He asks, "If your name is Jack of Teviotdale, then why does the maiden call you Robin?" He grips the hilt of his sword and draws it from its scabbard.

You steal a quick glance at Marian. Her eyes widen, and her hand covers her mouth in shock.

The first guard studies you for a moment, and then a smile spreads across his face. He turns and shouts, "Alert the Sheriff! We've captured Robin Hood!"

Little John rushes behind the guard and uses his staff to strike him. The guard falls to the ground. His sword clatters beside him.

"Come," Little John says. "Let's go!"

The second guard draws his weapon. "Halt!"

More guards charge through the crowd. You and your trusted companion begin to run toward the safety of the woods.

"Robin, behind you!" cries Marian. Her voice is filled with alarm.

You stop and turn, readying yourself for an attack. But before you can react, a guard's sword slides into your stomach. Pain sears through you. Your knees grow weak, and you fall to the dirt.

Marian appears beside you, on her knees. She cradles your head in her arms, and she sobs. You feel your life flowing from you. It is a welcome escape from the pain. You lie there, motionless, as darkness swallows you.

Go to page 67.

5

The Rescue of Will Stutely

Returning to camp, you tell the Merry Men of your adventure and of Will's unknown fate. Then you rest beneath the limbs of an oak tree and think of Will.

Two men hurry down the forest path. A woman is between them, an apron around her waist. She is from the Blue Boar—Eadom's wife, Maken.

Through gasping breath, one of the men calls out, "Will Stutely has been taken."

"He wasn't killed?" you ask, your voice filled with hope for your friend.

Maken shakes her head. "Eadom saw it all. He fears your man is wounded, for the deputy struck him hard upon his head. But he is alive."

Thank heavens. If Will is alive, there's a chance of saving him.

"Have they taken him to Nottingham?" you ask.

"Yes. He is to be executed tomorrow."

You shake your head. "He shall not die tomorrow if we Merry Men have anything to say about it!"

From your belt, you draw forth the horn and blow three loud blasts. In response, the entire band gathers around you.

"Will Stutely is alive, taken by that vile Sheriff!" you cry. "Will has risked life and limb for us many times. We ought to risk life and limb for him. Is it not so, Merry Men?"

The outlaw camp resounds with a hearty, "Aye!"

"Rest well, then. Tomorrow we'll take our blades to Nottingham and rescue our friend!"

Go to the next page.

The new dawn arrives. You and the Merry Men all travel through Sherwood Forest to the gray castle gates of Nottingham.

When all are gathered, you speak. "Time runs short. Let's get into town and mix ourselves with the people there. Keep one another in sight, and strike no man without need. We'll rescue Will and return to Sherwood together. No one gets left behind."

You walk the streets of Nottingham, disguised as a beggar with Little John at your side. The sun is low in the western sky when a horn sounds from the castle wall. Then, all of a sudden, crowds fill the streets. The castle gates open, and a great army of men enters with noise and clatter. The Sheriff, clad in armor, rides at the head. In the midst of the guard, Will Stutely rides in a prisoner cart.

You press closer to get a better look. When he is ten strides from you, a commotion stirs at the front of the army. The cart carrying Will creaks to a stop. You crane your neck to see what has stopped the riders.

A frightened boy, no more than five, lies fallen in the dirt before the Sheriff's horse.

The angered Sheriff shouts, "Remove him at once!"

No one steps forward to claim the boy.

You look to Little John. No one is paying attention to the cart. Using this distraction to free Will will be a simple matter. But the child's life might be in danger. Should you help the boy? Or is it wiser to free Will first? What will you choose to do?

To help the boy, go to page 90.

To rescue Will, go to page 99.

You're an outlaw, a wanted man. You must be careful not to trust anyone—especially a stranger.

"I fear you've traveled this far for nothing, lad," you say, clapping the messenger on the shoulder. "I will not leave Sherwood Forest."

The boy's eyes widen. He stutters as he says, "But . . . but sir, our King commands it."

"Send him my respect, but tell him I suspected a trap." With this said, you motion to Will, who promptly leads the boy back to his horse.

Will wraps the blindfold over the boy's eyes, then assists him onto his saddle. He leads the messenger back along the trail. The messenger's protests echo throughout the forest, eventually fading away as he disappears from sight.

Go to the next page.

Over the coming days, life in Sherwood returns to normal. On a morning when the sky is gray, you find yourself splitting logs for firewood. As you wipe sweat from your brow, you see one of your men—David of Doncaster—walking along the path toward camp. He is not alone; a woman walks beside him.

You drop your axe. "Marian!"

You dash toward her, and when she sees you, her eyes grow wide. You hug Marian tightly as she cries against your chest.

"I found her at the Blue Boar," David says. "She was looking for you." He bows and then leaves the two of you alone.

You whisper into Marian's ear. "What is it, Marian? What's wrong? Why have you come here?"

Marian begins to mumble. At first, you cannot make out the words. But then you hear, "I'm sorry, Robin. I'm so sorry. You must forgive me."

You draw her back, suddenly alert. "Forgive you for what?"

"For leading me here!" The Sheriff's cold voice echoes across the treetops.

You turn to find him at the camp's edge. His eyes are wild, and his hair is an unruly mess.

Then, suddenly, the forest is alive with soldiers. Armed against you with bows, swords, and axes, they smash through the underbrush and surround the camp.

You are weaponless, but you shield Marian with your body. Around you, the Merry Men are also caught unarmed. The Sheriff has you, and he knows it. With a wicked laugh, he raises his hand, and his men ready their weapons. Many of them point in your direction.

"Stay behind me," you whisper to Marian.

"Until my dying breath," she answers.

"Attack!" the Sheriff cries.

His men cheer as they crash forward, into the camp. You close your eyes as the Sheriff's bowmen release their shots. Fortunately, you barely have time to feel pain as the arrows hit their target.

Go to page 67.

You don't have time to rest—not when Marian's life is at risk. You lean forward and whisper to your horse, "Ride swiftly, and soon you will rest."

The horse gallops onward, but its legs begin to tremble from exhaustion. Then, suddenly, the horse trips, and you fall hard to the ground.

The horse lands solidly, whinnying. It rolls onto its back, and you are pinned beneath its bulk. Pain erupts along your left side, stemming forth from your leg and into your hip. Your head strikes the stone path, and your mind swims in a cloud of black.

And then there is nothing.

Go to page 67.

Marian's shouts are drawing attention. You have no choice but to turn on your heels and stride to her. Without a word, you slide your arm around her and kiss her.

Marian is startled by your sudden embrace, but her surprise quickly vanishes. Her fingers grasp your arms. "I knew you were alive."

"I wish that I could take you with me, but it's too dangerous. Do you understand?"

"Yes," she answers sadly.

"I'll return for you one day soon," you promise.

From the corner of your eye, you notice the guards. They begin walking through the crowd, toward you.

"I'm sorry," you tell Marian. "I must go."

A peasant walks past you, pulling a wagon. You quickly duck behind it, and you remain hidden until you reach the gate. Little John walks forward and steps in back of you to further hide your escape.

"Who was that fair maiden?" he asks quietly.

"The love of my life," you say.

You reach the road, and the other Merry Men join you. You glance back into the crowd, where the guards search about. Marian is nowhere to be seen.

That night, the Merry Men hold a feast in honor of your victory. Long into the night, you laugh and sing.

"You've done well," Little John says. "The arrow will earn many sacks of flour and vegetables. A good number of poor will eat this winter, thanks to you."

"A deed to be proud of," you answer. "Today, I heard the Sheriff speak of the 'coward' Robin Hood—that I dared not show my face at the shooting match. I wish to let him know the truth, to prove that I'm no coward."

Little John thinks for a moment, then says, "Take me and Will Stutely, and we'll send the Sheriff this news."

Go to the next page.

And so, by cover of moonlight, you walk back to Nottingham. You remain just outside the gates of town. Along the west wall, candlelight flickers from a window high in the brick. It's the Sheriff's room.

Crouching low, you remove an arrow from your quiver. You also pull out a rolled piece of scroll paper. In the dim blue moonlight, you read the words upon it:

Heaven Bless Thy Grace this day
Say all in sweet Sherwood
For the golden prize has been given away
To merry Robin Hood

You roll the scroll tightly around the arrow. Then you string the arrow and shoot. It sails upward, through the window. There is a clatter of dishes.

A moment passes as you wait in the bushes. Then a mighty voice calls out into the night. "Where did this come from?" the Sheriff screeches.

Little John chuckles. "Your point is made."

You laugh. "Let's return home."

4
A Risky Endeavor

Fall arrives. There's a crispness in the air. Wagons carrying winter supplies ride along the North Road often. The Merry Men choose only the richest of wagons to raid, and the mound of treasures hidden in Sherwood Forest grows.

You, Little John, and a round fellow named Friar Tuck lead your men and women into nearby towns. You provide sacks of food to the needy and the sick.

On one of these visits, a tavern owner named Eadom tells you, "The Sheriff's search for you has strengthened."

"How so?" you ask.

"A pair of the King's Guard was here three days ago. They spoke of a meeting between the Sheriff and his men. He ordered them to search the forest in groups of five. They're hiding at different points, waiting for you or your men to come across them."

"No one enters Sherwood that we can't find," Will Stutely boasts.

Eadom shrugs. "This may be so, but there's a bounty on your head, Robin."

"How much am I worth?"

"One hundred pounds of silver if you're brought to the Sheriff—dead or alive."

With this surprising news, you and the others walk back toward camp. The sounds of horse hooves and wagon wheels come from ahead, so you lead the others off the path.

A small caravan of riders, four in all, moves along the winding road. The last horseman pulls a wagon of valuable goods. You want to leap out and claim the wagon's treasures. Its contents would do well for the villagers.

You begin to stand, but Little John grabs your arm. "Stop," he whispers. "By taking this wagon, we could be alerting the Sheriff to our presence."

It's a fair concern. Is this a risk worth taking? The valuables on the wagon would help many. Should you confront the riders or remain hidden? What will you choose to do?

To take the wagon, go to page 102.

To stay in hiding, go to page 110.

Will Stutely has saved your life time and again. You will not abandon him. "I'm going nowhere, friend," you tell him. "We'll fight together."

You spot an elderly man sitting near you. A walking stick leans against his table. It isn't an ideal weapon, but it will have to do. You reach over and snatch the make-shift staff.

"Are you ready?" Will asks.

You nod.

A thin smile crosses his lips. Then Will leaps up, knocking over his wooden chair. The deputy pushes past Eadom and draws his sword. He charges toward you, but Will meets him with a blade of his own.

The guards block the door, their swords in hand. The walking stick is your only defense against them. Lucky for you, you've learned excellent skills from Little John.

You spin the weapon overhead and bring it down upon the helmet of the nearest guard. Two more men approach. You quickly kneel, swiping at the guards' feet and knocking them back. One drops his sword, and you swiftly grab it.

You pass the walking stick back to its owner. "Here you are, my good man," you say. "It's a fine stick."

As you turn back toward the battle, you spy Will looking in your direction. He points over your shoulder. "Robin, behind you!"

You turn, raising the sword. Metal clashes and sings as a guard strikes. Then the tavern door bursts open, and more of the Sheriff's men enter.

You have no option but to attack. You rush at the guards, who ready their blades. But there are too many of them. This battle will not end in your favor, and you know it. You made a poor choice. Because of it, today is the day you die.

Go to page 67.

Guy of Gisbourne gives you but a moment to decide before he leaps upon you. You throw down your bow and pluck the blade from the ground. There is just enough time to drop to one knee and raise the weapon before metal strikes against metal. The loud clang sends shivers down your arm.

You shove Guy of Gisbourne away and stagger to your feet. "You're surrounded," you tell him. "To even think you have a chance is foolish."

"Ha! Who else will stand against me?" he boasts. "Your men are engaged in battles of their own."

He pivots and swings his blade, but you quickly react. Guy of Gisbourne strikes at you, again and again. And each time, you protect yourself.

Your arms and shoulders ache with strain. You know that you cannot last much longer, but no Merry Men come to your aid. They wage their own battles.

At last, Guy of Gisbourne lands a good, strong blow that drives the breath from you. You fall to your knees, gasping for air.

"You put up a good fight," Guy of Gisbourne sneers. "But you've lost. I suggest you remain down."

You have no choice but to obey. Your strength is drained, and your arms hang limp at your sides.

"Look at me," Guy of Gisbourne says. "Let me see your face as I finish you, outlaw."

You gaze up at your opponent. To your surprise, something strikes him hard upon the side of his head. Guy of Gisbourne gives a yelp of pain. The item falls to his feet, and you see it's a half-eaten apple.

"Leave him alone!" shouts a tiny voice. The small boy, the one you saved from the Sheriff, has come to your defense. He stands at the front of the crowd.

Guy of Gisbourne laughs. "Run along, child!"

Another hurled object hits Guy of Gisbourne. This one, a large rock, causes him to stumble.

More peasants and townspeople grab stones from the ground and throw them at Guy of Gisbourne. Dozens of times, he is struck and wounded, until he can no longer bear the onslaught.

"This town has gone mad!" he shouts.

Guy of Gisbourne dashes for the castle. The Sheriff's remaining men follow him, leaving everyone—including Will—behind.

You rise slowly, watching as Little John hurries to check on Will. You go to the boy, kneel, and place your hand on his shoulder. "Many thanks," you say. "Even the smallest of us can make a difference." You stand and address the crowd. "Many thanks to you all!"

Go to page 119.

"What are you waiting for?" Will hisses.

You do not wish to leave Will, but you have no choice. Perhaps when you're outside, with more space to fire your bow, you can draw attention away from the tavern and your friend.

"Do you remember the place we met?" you ask.

Will nods.

"Meet me there."

"I'll do my best not to keep you waiting in that dark cave, friend."

Will jumps up, knocking over his wooden chair and drawing the guards' attentions. The deputy reaches for his sword and charges. But Will is prepared to do battle, and their swords clang together.

You dash across the room, bursting through the heavy oak door with all of your strength.

A guard shouts, "The other escapes!"

You do not halt. The forest is only a few strides ahead of you, but the sound of horse hooves stops you. You turn in time to see a rider behind you. He lifts his sword and swings it. You drop to the ground as the blade sweeps over your head.

You quickly shed the cloak, freeing your bow. You string an arrow and shoot. It slices across the guard's arm, forcing him to drop his sword.

Three more horsemen round the stone building with weapons drawn. They ride fast toward you.

Sounds of battle continue inside the tavern. Will is a strong fighter. You pray that he finds his way to the cave unharmed.

You race into the woods before the Sheriff's men can follow. You run swiftly for several minutes, until you're sure that you've eluded the King's Guard.

When you reach the river, you kneel on the rocks and cup handfuls of cool water into your mouth. Your hands steady and your head clears.

Following the winding riverbanks, you reach the cave in good time. You do not bother to hide. Instead, you sit on the fallen log and wait. You are hungry and devour your sack of dried meats.

Once, you hear the sound of snapping twigs along the path, so you crouch behind the fallen log. But it is not Will who approaches; it's a deer. The creature bounds off into the underbrush.

Time passes. The sun reaches its midday peak, then descends back toward the earth. Still, there is no sign of Will. You hold out hope for his safe return. But as sunset darkens Sherwood Forest, you come to a terrible realization: Will has either been captured or killed.

Go to page 124.

With Marian's life in danger, the choice is simple. You will take all of the help you can get. Bowing your head to the King, you say, "I'm yours to command."

King Richard smiles, claps your shoulder, and says, "You'll ride with fifty of my finest men to Sherwood. You'll end this plot before your maiden is harmed."

And so, by the light of the afternoon sun, you ride out of London. The King's royal guardsmen follow you into the wilds.

Go to the next page.

For four days, you ride, resting only a few hours each night. At last, you pass into Sherwood Forest. By the time you reach the edge of camp, Little John and Will are waiting for you.

"You've brought guests," Little John says. "I'm not sure we have enough green for all of them to wear."

You aren't in a joking mood. After dismounting, you explain the Sheriff's plot.

"What will you have us do?" asks Little John.

"Prepare the camp for the Sheriff's attack. Each man shall be armed at all times. The Sheriff will use Marian to find us. And when he does find us, we'll be ready."

For seven long days, you remain in camp, while the King's Guard hide nearby. Finally, on the eighth day, you see one of your men—David of Doncaster—walking along the path toward camp. He is not alone; a woman walks beside him.

"Marian!" you shout excitedly.

You dash toward her, and when she sees you, her eyes grow wide. You hug Marian tightly, as she cries against your chest.

"I found her at the Blue Boar," David says. "She was looking for you." He bows and then leaves the two of you alone.

You whisper into Marian's ear. "What is it, Marian? What's wrong?"

Marian begins to mumble. At first, you cannot make out the words. But then you hear, "I'm sorry, Robin. I'm so sorry. You must forgive me."

You lean close to her ear and whisper, "I know."

Suddenly, the forest is alive with soldiers. Armed with bows, swords, and axes, they smash through the underbrush and surround the camp. At their lead is the Sheriff, whose madness shows in his unruly hair and wild eyes. Guy of Gisbourne stands beside him.

"Here it is!" the Sheriff cries. "The home of Robin Hood and his Merry Men!"

You place yourself between the Sheriff and Marian, but you do not draw your bow. Today, you wield a sword given to you by the King. It is marked with the King's royal symbol, which you want the Sheriff to see.

He does, asking, "Have you robbed the new King?"

"No," you answer. "Our days as outlaws are done."

You blow the bugle with three sharp breaths, and the King's Guard emerge from their places of hiding.

The camp goes still. Each side awaits the other's attack. The first to make a move will have an advantage. But if neither side begins, perhaps this battle can be avoided. Will you attack first? Or should you wait to see what the Sheriff does? What will you choose to do?

To attack, go to page 96.

To wait, go to page 100.

Epilogue:
A Good Deed

The blast of a sharp whistle startles you. Your eyes snap open. You look around the subway station; no one is paying you any attention. The digital clock on the wall reads 3:45 p.m. You hear a subway car rattling toward the station—your ride.

You look down and see that your hands are empty. Where's the book? Was it ever there? Or was your entire adventure nothing but a dream?

It doesn't matter. Something inside you has changed. Without a second thought, you hop off the bench. You don't have much time, so you must be quick.

You dart between pedestrians, snaking your way across the platform, until you reach the man asking for change. You feel bad to think that he's down on his luck. You reach into your pocket and take out your money. Then you lean forward and place it inside his chipped mug.

The man nods. "Thank you."

You smile. "You're welcome."

With a small wave, you rush across the platform again, reaching the train just as it screeches to a stop. Its doors open, and you climb aboard. As you find a seat, you wonder what the world would be like if everyone cared more about those in need. The thought hangs with you as the subway begins to move, speeds up, and takes you on your way home.

Go to the next page.

The End

You have
survived the
Merry Adventures
of Robin Hood!

CAN YOU SURVIVE THESE STORIES?

Test your survival skills with a free
short story at **www.Lake7Creative.com**,
and pick up these Choose Your Path books:

- *Bram Stoker's Dracula*

- *Greek Mythology's Adventures of Perseus*

- *Jack London's Call of the Wild*

- *Jules Verne's 20,000 Leagues Under the Sea*

- *Sir Arthur Doyle's Adventures of Sherlock Holmes*

About Howard Pyle

Howard Pyle was an author and illustrator. He was born in 1853 in Wilmington, Delaware. As an adult, he worked as an illustration professor at Drexel Institute of Art, Science, and Industry (now Drexel University). He later founded his own school, the Howard Pyle School of Illustration Art. Many of his students went on to become famous illustrators. Mr. Pyle created numerous illustrations of pirates, and he is credited with creating the now-common image of pirate clothing.

As an author, Mr. Pyle is best known for adapting the ballads of Robin Hood for young readers. *The Merry Adventures of Robin Hood* was published in 1883. He also adapted a four-volume set of books about King Arthur and wrote many other stories with medieval settings.

Mr. Pyle died while studying mural paintings in Florence, Italy, in 1911. Today, he is still commonly remembered as the "father of American illustration."

About His Book

Was Robin Hood a real person? Maybe, but nobody knows for sure. His legend was first told in ballads, or stories sung to music. (Books were not common back then, so ballads made stories easier to remember and retell.) The earliest known Robin Hood ballad was sung in the early 15th century, although his tales usually took place alongside King Richard the Lionheart, a real king who ruled England in the late 12th century.

In 1883, author/illustrator Howard Pyle collected the traditional ballads about the famous outlaw. He wove them together and turned them into a book. Mr. Pyle's *The Merry Adventures of Robin Hood* was aimed at young readers. It helped to make Robin Hood one of the most famous characters in history.

This Choose Your Path version of Mr. Pyle's *Robin Hood* focuses on a few of the best-known ballads. But Pyle's text also includes many other stories about the famous outlaw. It is with deep respect for Mr. Pyle's work that we present this adaptation.

About the Author

When Brandon Terrell was a boy, he wanted to grow up to be an adventurer. (Okay, he still does!) Many of his childhood memories include reading. His favorite books were mysteries and action-packed tales. One of his favorite characters was Robin Hood. He imagined himself running through the forest, bow in hand, ready to face the evil Sheriff of Nottingham.

While archery is not among Brandon's talents, he is the author of numerous books, including chapter books, picture books, and graphic novels. He lives in Saint Paul, Minnesota, with his wife, Jennifer, and their two children.